A Little Book of
Body Language

Vijaya Kumar

NEW DAWN PRESS, INC.
Chicago • Slough • New Delhi

NEW DAWN PRESS GROUP

Published by New Dawn Press Group
New Dawn Press, Inc., 244 South Randall Rd # 90, Elgin, IL 60123

New Dawn Press, 2 Tintern Close, Slough, Berkshire, SL1-2TB, UK

New Dawn Press (An Imprint of Sterling Publishers (P) Ltd.)
A-59, Okhla Industrial Area, Phase-II, New Delhi-110020

A Little Book of Body Language
Copyright © 2004, New Dawn Press
ISBN 1 932705 15 5
Reprint 2010

All rights are reserved. No part of this publication may be
reproduced, stored in a retrieval system or transmitted, in any form
or by any means, mechanical, photocopying, recording or otherwise,
without prior written permission of the original publisher.

NOTE FROM THE PUBLISHER

The author specifically disclaims any liability, loss or risk
whatsoever, which is incurred or likely to be incurred, as a
consequence of any direct or indirect use of information given
in this book. The contents of this work are a personal
interpretation of the subject by the author.

PRINTED IN INDIA

Contents

Introduction 5

What is Body Language? 7

Facial Expressions and Hand Gestures 13

Palm Gestures 15

Hand and Arm Gestures 26

Hand-to-Face Gestures 37

Limb Barriers 47

Eye Signals 57

Other Popular Gestures 62

Attitudes 72

Courtship Gestures 75

Territorial and Ownership Gestures 80

Mirror Images 83

Pointers 85

Influence of Spatial Zone and Culture on Body Language 92

Conclusion 95

Introduction

This book aims to make the reader aware of his body language—his own non-verbal gestures and signals—and understand the gesture and communicative signals of his fellow beings. The acquisition of knowledge and adeptness at non-verbal communication, makes every encounter with another person, a thrilling experience. One learns to read others' thoughts by their gestures and have an exciting time just watching their body language rituals! One can, with perception and intuition, tell, if someone is lying, or trying to impress someone, or else, is simply bored! Read on, and learn more about the body language which speaks volumes!

Please note that wherever the pronouns he and his have been used, implication has been drawn to both males and females.

What is Body Language?

Body language is the unique non-verbal channel of communication, by which we convey information, or express ourselves through conscious or subconscious gestures, body movements, and facial expressions. This means of communication can be a deliberate replacement for our speech, a reinforcement to it, or a reflector or a concealer of our mood.

Body language comprises body gestures and verbal signals.

Many signals are inborn, some are learned, others are genetically transferred, or acquired in different ways. A person may stand in a particular style which could be genetic or inborn. On the other hand, a gesture can be cultural, eg shrugging which is so common to the Americans that it is identified with their culture.

The Basics

Most of the basic communication gestures are similar worldwide. People laugh when happy or amused, cry when sad and frown or glare when angry. Nodding the head indicates affirmation or 'yes'. 'No' is indicated by shaking one's head from side to side.

When one is in doubt, or does not understand what another person is saying, one may simply shrug one's shoulders. The shoulder shrug is commonly depicted by exposed palms, hunched shoulders and raised brows.

Sometimes, however, a gesture which has a specific significance for one culture, may have an altogether different meaning for another, e.g., the thumb-up, the V-sign, or the ring gesture.

Cluster of Gestures

It would be wrong for a novice to interpret a single gesture without taking other gestures and circumstances into consideration. For example, scratching the head could mean forgetfulness, uncertainty, lying, dandruff, sweating or fleas, depending on the other gestures accompanying it.

Body language consists of words, sentences and punctuations too. Each gesture is like a word which may have various connotations, and when put together with other words, forms a sentence which helps one get the full meaning, and irrevocably reveals a person's feelings or attitudes.

For an accurate interpretation of body language, one has to keenly observe a cluster of gestures and the similarity of the verbal and non-verbal channels of communication.

Study of Gestures in Context

All gestures should be studied in the context in which they appear. A person sitting huddled at a hilltop on a cold winter day must be crossing his arms and legs tightly to keep himself warm, while the same person sitting in that same posture in front of a sales executive who is trying to sell him a product may be on the defensive or may be uninterested.

Similarly, a person with ill-fitting clothes may be unable to use certain gestures which can affect his body language. So, one has to also consider a person's disabilities or physical handicaps that may hinder his body movements.

Status and Power

Studies reveal that the higher the position of a person in society, the better he is able to communicate in words and phrases.

A person's command over the spoken word is correlated with the volume of gestures that he makes to communicate his message. While a person with status and power can communicate effectively with words, the less skilled one uses more gestures than words to get the message across. With age, a person's actions become more refined and less obvious, hence, making it difficult for the gestures to be read accurately.

A young child covers his mouth soon after lying, with one or both hands. This habit may continue in his adult life, with just the speed of the action slowing down.

A teenager, when lying, might also bring his hands to his mouth, but instead of clamping them on it, he will rub his fingers lightly around his mouth. In adulthood, this gesture transforms thus: the hand nears the mouth, lands under the nose and rubs it.

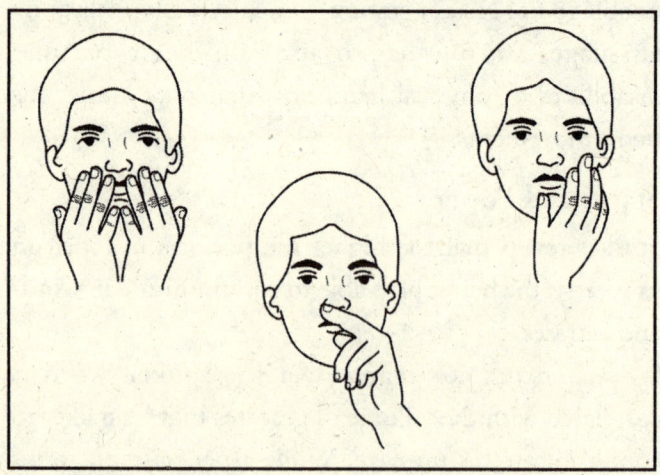

Gestures when lying

Faking Body Language

It is generally not possible to fake body language, because the body's microsignals would otherwise clash with spoken words.

An open palm denotes honesty. A man may hold his palms out as he smiles at you and lies, but his pupils may contract, one eyebrow maybe raised, or a corner of his mouth may twitch—these gestures contradict this open palm gesture.

Sometimes, for a short spell, one can fake body language to create a positive impact or impression, but this is only short-lived.

A person attending an interview may give all the signals which are not part of his natural gestures, but which could help him create an impressive image about himself.

The face, more than any other part of the body, is used to cover up a lie, but in such a situation there is no harmony between the facial and body gestures.

Telling Lies Successfully

It is very difficult to lie and get away with it, because our subconscious mind acts automatically and the gestures following it, give it away.

Good liars, like politicians, lawyers, actors, etc, have honed their body gestures to such skillful techniques that they can lie with straight faces and hoodwink others. They practise the right gestures that they think are correct when they tell a lie, and this does, indeed, need a lot of practice to be convincing.

Professional interviewers, sales people and very shrewd and perceptive people can, in fact, detect, through microgestures – like a facial twitch, contracting pupils, increased thinking, sweating at the brows, flushing of the cheeks, etc, – that a person is lying.

This is the reason why the police place the suspect on a chair under bright light, with his body in full view, at the time of interrogation.

Facial Expressions and Hand Gestures

The most visually expressive part of our body is the face. There are six universal facial expressions as discussed in the chart on page 14: happiness, sadness, surprise, fear, anger and distrust, and each of them is accompanied with a combination of recognisable signals. The table on the next page, will also provide a quick glance at our changing emotional gestures.

Apart from the fare, the hands are the most expressive. We use them to reinforce our speech or at times even as its replacement. In the next few chapters, with follow a combination of hand gestures, beginning with palm gestures and finger gestures and moving on to a comibination of hand, arm and face gestures.

Facial Expressions	Eyes and Eyebrows	Forehead	Nose	Cheeks	Mouth
1. Happiness	The lower eyelids rise slightly, wrinkles appearing below them and the eyes become narrower.			Rise and bulge	Lips part and mouth lengthens sometimes to show teeth.
2. Sadness	Inner end of eyebrows may rise. Eyes may glisten with tears.	Wrinkles may appear			Droops at the corners and lips may quiver.
3. Surprise	Eyebrows curve upwards and eyes open wide.				Jaws drop and mouth opens slackly.
4. Fear	Upper eyelids rise, exposing the whites of the eyes, and lower eyelids tense and rise too.	Wrinkles furrow			Lips pull back.
5. Anger	Eyebrows pull inward and upper, and lower eyelids move closer.		Some flare their nostrils		Lips close tightly.
6. Disgust	Lower eyelids rise and wrinkles appear below them.		Wrinkles	Move up	Both lips rise or only upper lip rises and lower lip lowers to form a pout.

Palm Gestures

Apart from the face, the hands are the most expressive. We use them to reinforce our speech or at times even as its replacement.

Open Palm Gesture

The *open palm* denotes truth, openness, faithfulness and compliance. The *palm is placed over the heart* while taking an oath, held in the air when giving evidence in a court of law, or placed on a holy book while standing witness in a court.

- The two basic palm positions are the *palm facing upward*, and the *palm facing downward*. In the *upward-facing position*, a person may be begging for something, as in the case of a beggar, and in the downward-facing position, he may be trying to hold down or constrain something.
- When a person wishes to be totally open and honest, he holds out one or both palms to the other person with the *palms exposed*, and expresses his wish to be frank with him.
- A child may *hide his palms* behind him when he is lying or hiding something.

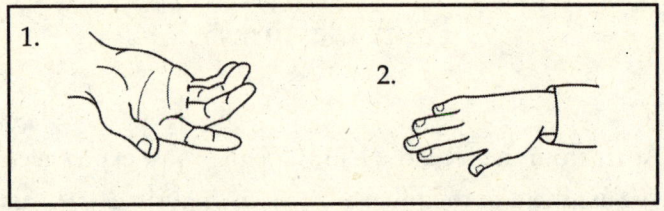

1. Upward-facing palm;   2. Downward-facing palm

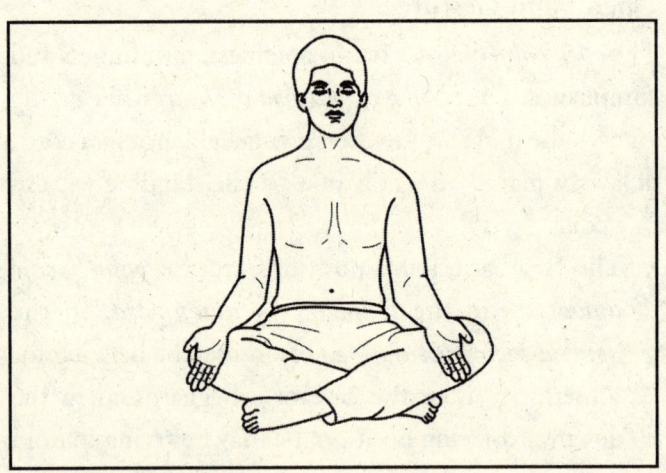

Open palm gesture

- A husband may either hold his *palms together* or have them in his pockets when he is trying to explain to his wife why he was out so late at night, the hidden palms indicating to the wife that he is holding back the truth.
- A shrewd salesman will realise that the customer is genuinely not interested in his product when he notices the open palm gesture of his client.

Palm Power Gesture

There are three main palm command gestures—*palm-up, palm-down, palm-closed-finger-pointed* positions.

- The *palm-up* signifies submission, a non-threatening gesture.
- The *palm-down* position denotes authority and depending upon the relationship between a worker and his senior, the situation could be explosive or just routine.
- In the *palm-closed-finger-pointed* position, the speaker compels his listener into submission.

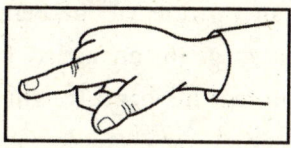

Pointing a finger

- One of the most irritating and annoying gestures is to see the speaker *pointing a finger* at you, and beating time or punctuating his words with it.

A habitual finger-pointer, will learn to create a more relaxed attitude, with a positive effect on people, if he only learns to use the palm-up or palm-down positions more often.

Handshakes

The age-old custom of shaking hands, practised even today, involves the interlocking and shaking of the palms.

In English-speaking countries, the handshake gesture is used both during the initial greeting and during departure. During such handshakes, the hands are generally pumped five to seven times.

While shaking hands, one of the following three basic attitudes is conveyed—*dominance, submission* or *equality*.

- When your *palm faces upward*, submission is denoted. For example, an arthritic patient, being weak, can be submissive; a surgeon, an artist, or a musician, wanting to protect his hand, might be submissive too.

- Dominance is conveyed when your *palm faces down* in the handshake, in relation to the other person's palm.

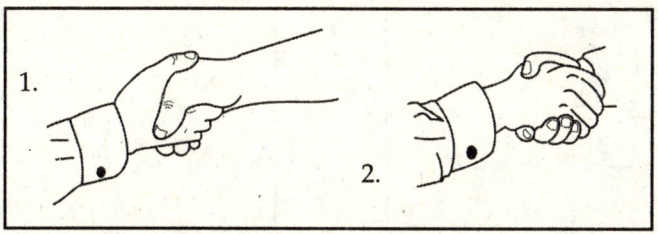

1. Submissive handshake; 2. Dominant handshake

- Two dominant people shaking hands would like to see the other submissive, hence there is every likelihood of the hands being held in a *vice-like grip*.

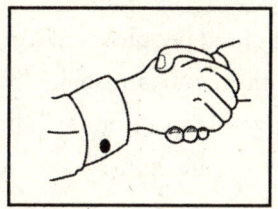

Handshake

- In order to intimidate the other dominant person, *step forward with your left foot* as you reach to shake hands, then *bringing your right foot forward*, place it *in his personal space*, then *bring your left foot beside the other foot,* and *shake the person's hand.* This allows you to take command, by invading the other person's personal space.

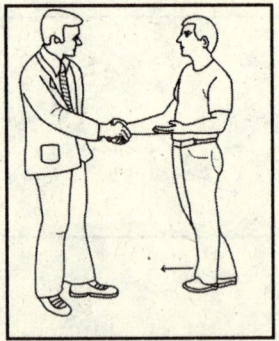

Bringing your right foot forward

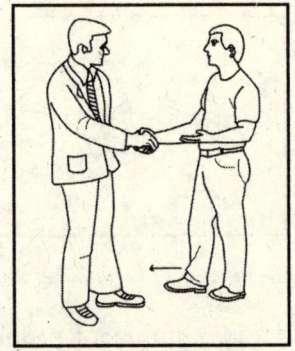

Entering the personal space

- Most right-handed people are at a disadvantage when they get a dominant handshake, for they have very little manoeuvrable space or flexibility to move within the confines of the handshake, letting the other person gain mastery.
- Another way to dominate the other person, is to *grasp the person's hand on top and then shake it,* for then your hand, which will be in a *palm facing down* position, is in a superior position on top of his. This, of course, should be done judiciously and cautiously.

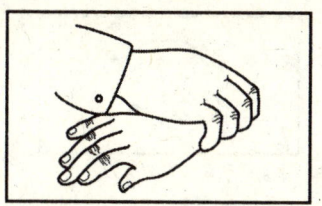
Grasping the person's hand on top

- Though, a handshake is a sign of welcome, sales people are taught that if they initiate the handshake with a buyer on whom they have called without appointment, the result could be negative as the buyer may not want to receive them.
- The *glove handshake*, sometimes called the politicians' handshake, creates suspicion and caution in the receiver's mind when he is meeting the initiator for the first time. This kind of handshake should be used with only known people.

Glove handshake

- The *dead-fish handshake* is an uninviting greeting gesture. The clammy, cold feeling, like that of touching a dead fish, relates it to weak-charactered people, making this type of handshake unpopular.

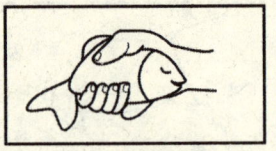

Dead-fish handshake

- The *knuckle-grinder handshake* leaves you wanting to hit out at the other person.

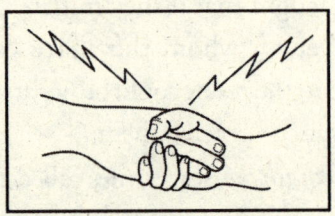

Knuckle-grinder handshake

- The *stiff-arm thrust* in a handshake is special to aggressive types, the main purpose being to keep the receiver at a distance, and not allow him to enter his personal space. The stiff-arm thrust is usually used by people residing in the country where they have a larger intimate zone to protect.

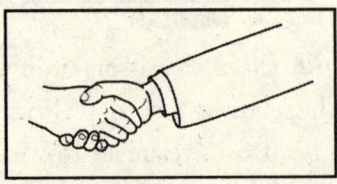

Stiff-arm thrust

- In the *fingertip-grab*, the person mistakenly grabs the receiver's fingers, showing that he lacks confidence, though appearing to be eager. The fingertip handshake is also used when the person wants to keep the other at a safe distance.

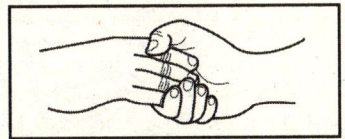

Fingertip-grab

- A person who tends to pull the other's palm during a handshake does so either because he feels safe only in his zone, or because he hails from a culture that has a small intimate zone, and so is behaving normally.

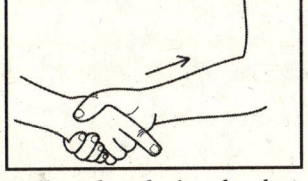

Pulling the other's palm during a handshake

- The *double-handed handshake* signifies trust and sincerity towards the receiver.

In the *double-handed clasp*, the left hand on the wrist, the elbow, the upper arm, or the shoulder, transmits more feeling than the palm, i.e., the further he moves his palm up the receiver's arm, the more feeling he wishes to communicate.

- Only when one is sure of mutual feelings, should one use the double-handed shake, else the receiver will be suspicious of his intentions.

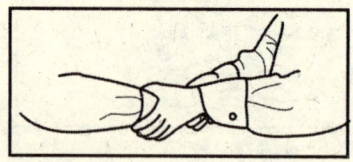

Wrist-hold

- The *wrist-hold and the elbow-grasp* is generally used between friends or relatives, where the user's left hand penetrates the receiver's intimate zone.
- The *upper-arm and shoulder-grasp* also signifies the initiator's entry into the receiver's close, intimate zone, and may also involve body contact.

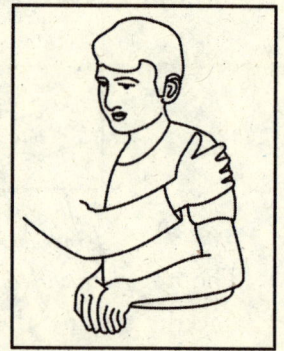

Shoulder-hold

Rubbing Palms Together

Rubbing the palms together *denotes some positive expectations* from the doer. For example, the master of ceremonies, or a dice thrower, or a magician, rubs his palms in anticipation of something positive.

- The *speed at which a person rubs his palms together* suggests that he expects the other person to benefit. For example if someone goes to a car dealer and describes what he is looking for, the dealer rubs his palms together quickly, and says that he has the right car for him. The signal here is that the dealer expects the buyer to benefit.
- If you *rub your palms very slowly*, then the message that the other person gets is that you are *crafty or devious*, and applied to the car dealer-buyer example, the buyer would think that he is not going to benefit and that the dealer would be benefitting instead.

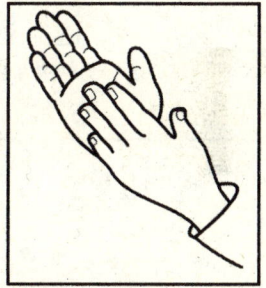

Rubbing palms

Hand and Arm Gestures

Hands Clenched Together

Hands that are clenched together are generally indicative of frustration or hostility, or holding back a negative attitude. This gesture has three positions — *hands clenched in front of the face, hands clenched and resting on*

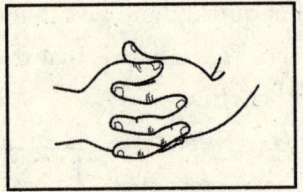
Hands clenched on desk

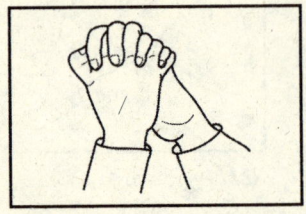
Hands clenched in raised position

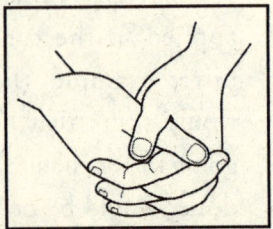
Hands clenched in lower position in front of crotch

a desk or on the lap, and *hands clenched together in a raised position*.

There is also a correlation between the height at which the hands are held and the strength of the person's negative mood. For example, it will be more difficult to handle a person whose hands are held together in a raised position than the person whose hands are clenched on the desk.

In order to ease the hostile attitude of a person with clenched hands, ways have to be devised to unlock the person's hands to expose the palms and the front of the body.

Steepling Hands

Steepling is often used and studied individually — separately from other gestures.

Superior, confident individuals whose body gestures are minimal, often use this gesture, denoting their confident attitude — eg managers, accountants, lawyers, etc

This gesture has two types — the *raised steeple* and the *lowered steeple*.

- When the person concerned is talking and giving his ideas and opinions, he normally adopts the *raised steeple gesture*.

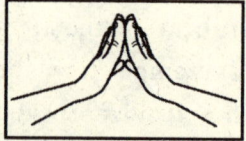

Raised steeple

- When the steepler is listening, he uses the *lowered steeple gesture*.

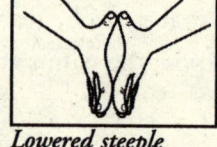

Lowered steeple

- Generally, women use the lowered steeple gesture more often than the raised one.
- When the steepler uses the *raised steeple gesture,* and also *tilts his head back,* he smacks of smugness or arrogance.
- The steeple gesture is a positive signal, but it can be misinterpreted under negative circumstances.

A potential buyer may have indicated some positive response by gestures like open palms, leaning forward, head up, etc In such a case, if the steeple gesture ensures a chain of negative gestures like arm-folding, leg-crossing, several hand-to-face gestures, the buyer will not hesitate to reject the deal, as he will be confident that he will not buy. In this case, the consequence will be negative for the salesman.

Hand, Arm and Wrist Grips

- When a person has *one palm gripping the other hand behind his back*, he exudes confidence and superiority. Military personnel, policemen patrolling the beat, the principal of a school walking through the school yard, etc, use this gesture.

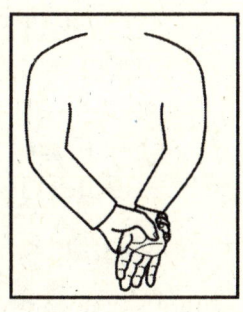

Confidence-Superiority Gesture

A person using this gesture exposes the front portion of his body to others in an act of fearlessness. This gesture helps one to relax in highly tense situations.

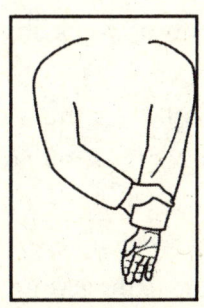

Above the wrist gripping gesture

- When a person grips *one hand tightly with the other, above the wrist and behind his back*, he denotes frustration which he is attempting to control, as if to prevent the other hand from striking out.

- When the *gripping hand moves further up the other hand*, it indicates that the person is extremely angry, and shows a greater attempt at self-control than the person gripping the arm just above the wrist. This gesture is commonly seen in salesmen who are asked to wait indefinitely.

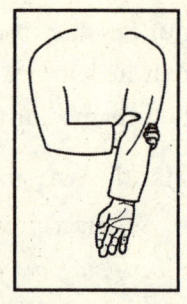

Upper-arm gripping gesture

Thumb Displays

Thumbs denote strength of character and pride. They display superiority, dominance, and even aggression.

Thumb gestures are secondary gestures, being a supportive part of a cluster of gestures.

These gestures are positive, often used by managers in front of their subordinates, a courting man in the presence of a potential female partner, or people sporting high-status or prestige clothing.

People wearing new or attractive clothes use thumb gestures more frequently than those wearing older, outdated clothing.

The thumbs become more obvious when a person gives a verbal message that is contradictory to the gesture.

For example, a lawyer may address a jury in a soft voice, saying, "In my humble opinion, ladies and gentlemen of the jury", while holding his head back, and using dominant thumb gestures that belie his address to the jury, making him appear pompous.

Contradictory verbal and thumb signals

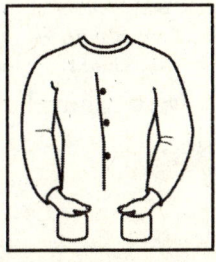

Pocket thruster with thumb out

- Thumbs most often stick out from people's pockets, and such *thumb thrusters* will often rock on the balls of their feet, trying to give an impression of extra height.

- Thumbs sometimes *protrude from back pockets* in a furtive or secretive manner, in order to hide the person's dominant manner.

Many women who are aggressive and very dominant, like to adopt male gestures and positions, and can be seen with their hands thrust in their pant pockets with thumbs protruding outside.

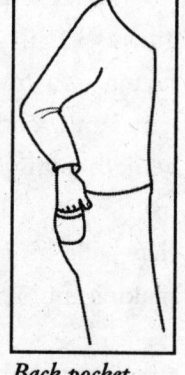

Back pocket thrust with thumb out

The dominant female

- When a person folds his arms, with his *thumbs pointing upwards*, he shows his defensive or negative attitude (arms crossed) plus a superior attitude, (thumbs protruding upward) gesturing with his thumbs, and rocking on the balls of his feet.

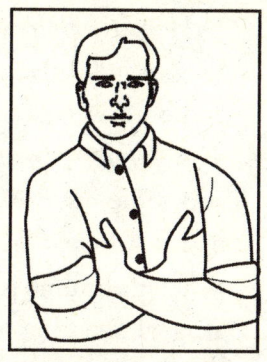

Thumbs-up, arms folded

- The *thumb, when pointing at another person*, can signal ridicule or disrespect.
- *Thumb-shaking* is less common among women, although they sometimes use this gesture for people they have no liking towards.

Thumb pointing at another person

- *Rubbing the thumb against the fingertips or the index finger* is indicative of money expectancy. Sales people and borrowers generally use this gesture.
- The *thumb-up gesture*, as practised in India, Britain and some other Commonwealth countries, is used by hitch-hikers thumbing a lift.
- When the thumb is jerked sharply upwards, indicates a signal denoting insult.
- In a few countries like Italy, counting on fingers starts with the thumb-up gesture, and takes the index finger as denoting number two. Strangely, in Australia, America and Britain, the counting starts from the index finger, denoting one, the middle finger two, and so on, while the thumb represents number five!

The Ring Gesture

Popularised in the US during the early nineteenth century by scribes, to shorten phrases, the ring gesture stands for *okay or all-correct*. The all-correct was probably spelt then as 'all correct', later shortened to OK.

Another theory bases it as the opposite of knockout—KO (OK).

Yet another view is that it is an abbreviation of Old Kinderbook, the birthplace of an American president in the nineteenth century, who used the initials 'OK' as a campaign slogan. Other meanings of 'OK':

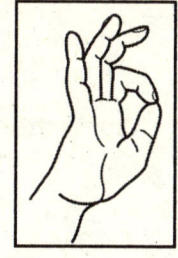
The ring gesture

- In Japan, the ring gesture means 'money'.
- In some Mediterranean countries, this sign indicates homosexuality.
- In France, it means 'zero' or 'nothing'.
- In some cities in India, especially in the south, it means 'well done' or 'top class' or 'A-one'.

The 'V' Sign

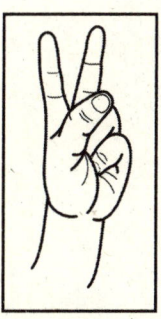
The 'V' sign

Winston Churchill used the 'V' sign gesture for victory during the second world war. In his version of this gesture, *the index and the middle finger were held up in the shape of a V, with his palm facing outward.*

- When the *palm faces towards the speaker and the relevant two fingers are held out* in the shape of a V, the gesture denotes an obscure insult.

- For many in Europe and in the South Asian countries, it means the number two.
- A bartender would give two mugs of bear if he was shown this gesture.

Hand-to-Face Gestures

The most common deceit signals that people give away are those depicted by the three wise monkeys who hear, speak and see no evil.

Hand-to-face gestures

Children use these obvious deceit gestures openly and very often. As children grow older, their hand-to-face gestures become more subtle and less obvious. These gestures mean doubt, uncertainty, lying or exaggeration.

It is important not to interpret hand-to-face gestures in isolation, but to also observe other clusters of gestures that may help you to confirm your suspicions of deceit or lying.

The Mouth Guard

This gesture, one of the few adult gestures, is as obvious as a child's gesture.

- This gesture involves *the hand covering the mouth, with the thumb pressed against a cheek,* implying that the person wishes to *suppress something being voiced.* Sometimes several fingers on a closed fist are used over the mouth in the gesture.

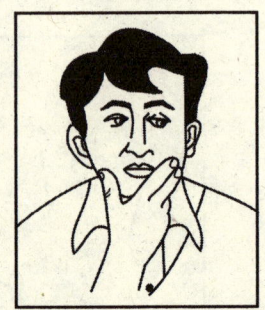

The mouth guard

- Some people camouflage their gesture by faking a cough.
- A person using this gesture while speaking is obviously telling a lie.
- On the other hand, if he uses this gesture when someone else is speaking, it indicates that he feels the other person is lying.

The Nose Touch

The nose touch is a disguised and more sophisticated version of the mouth guard.

- The gesture could be a *quick, light touch below the nose* or may be indicated by several *light rubs below the nose*.

The nose touch

- The reason for this gesture could be the spontaneous hand movement towards the mouth in response to some negative thoughts, but at the last minute, shifting the fingers under the nose.
- Like the mouth guard gesture, this gesture too can be used both by the speaker to *hide* his own *deceit*, and by the listener who doubts the speaker's words.

The Eye Rub

- When *men* lie, they *rub their eyes* vigorously. When the *lie is a big one*, they will often look away generally towards the floor.

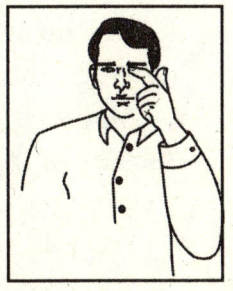

The eye rub

- *Women* who are mostly conscious of their looks, use a small, *gentle rub just below the eye.*
- Women also avoid making eye contact with the listener, preferring to look up at the ceiling.
- Movie actors who have to portray insincerity in movies, often use a cluster of gestures that include the eye rub, a false smile, clenched teeth and an averted gaze.

The Ear Rub

- When a *person wishes not to hear* what the other person is saying, he discreetly puts his *hand around or over the ear.*
- Young children show their naivete by putting both hands on both ears to shut out what they do not want to hear.

The ear rub

- When a person *pulls at his earlobe or bends the entire ear forward to cover the ear hole,* it indicates that *he has heard enough,* or may *want to speak.*

The Neck Scratch

This gesture has the *index finger rubbing the side of the neck or the area below the ear.* This gesture indicates *uncertainty or doubt,* and is generally used by a person who says, "I'm not sure I agree."

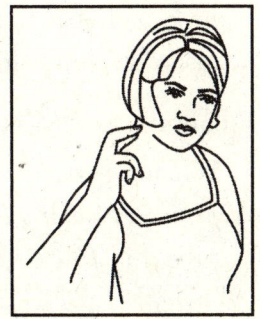

The neck scratch

- The person's doubtful attitude becomes obvious when his speech contradicts his gesture.

He may say, "I can understand how you feel", while scratching his neck—a gesture, which shows his uncertainty.

The Collar Pull

The collar pull

- When a person *tells a lie and suspects that he has been caught,* he tends to *pull his collar,* probably to ease the tingling sensation in his neck caused by the lie.

- This gesture is also used when a person is *angry or frustrated* and by *pulling at the collar away from the neck,* he hopes to allow cool air to circulate around his neck, thus calming himself down.

Fingers in the Mouth

- When a person is *under pressure,* he invariably puts his *fingers in his mouth.*
- Sometimes he is apt to put objects like a pen, a pencil, a cigarette, etc, into his mouth, unconsciously attempting to relieve his stress.

Fingers in the mouth

- This gesture is an external manifestation of an inner need for reassurance.

Cheek and Chin Gestures

- When a person *supports his head with his hand,* it indicates that he is *bored,* uninterested and is attempting to stave off sleep.

Boredom

- *Continual foot-tapping and drumming of fingers on the table* are not signs of boredom, but of *impatience.* The speed of the foot-tap or finger-drumming is in proportion to the extent of the person's impatience.
- A person shows *interested* evaluation when his *closed hand rests on his cheek with the index finger pointing upwards.*

Interested evaluation

Having negative thoughts

- When a person has *negative or critical thoughts,* his *thumb supports his chin, while his index finger points vertically up the cheek.*

- When a person is making a *decision,* his hand will move to the chin and begin a *chin-stroking gesture.* When a salesperson asks a buyer for his decision, if the buyer follows his chin-stroking gesture with the crossing of his arms and legs, sitting back in his chair, then the salesperson can be sure that the decision arrived at is a definite 'no'.

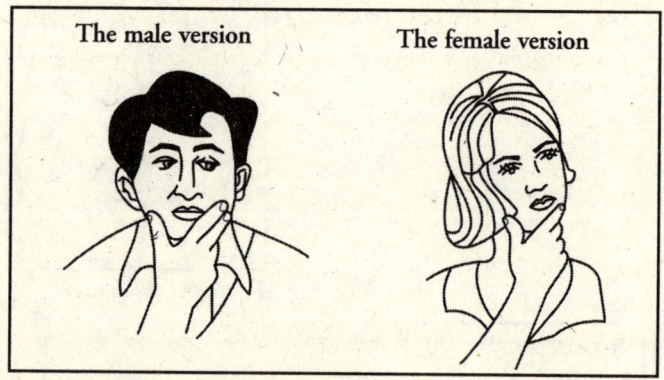

Making a decision

Decision-Making Gestures
- A person who wears glasses might be seen removing them from his face, and putting one end of the frame in his mouth instead of using the chin-stroking gesture.

- A pipe smoker might put his pipe in his mouth.
- A person may put his pencil end or pen, or even a fingertip in his mouth while making a decision. The object in his mouth suggests that he is unsure, and needs assurance in making a quick decision.
- When a person is making a decision, his hand may be stroking his chin, but as he begins to lose interest in the speaker, his head begins to rest on his chin.

Evaluation - decision making

Evaluation-boredom

Head-Rubbing and Head-Slapping Gestures

- Sometimes when a person is *lying*, instead of pulling his collar, he is seen *rubbing the back of his neck*, also called the pain-in-the-neck gesture. When using this gesture, he usually avoids your gaze and looks down.

- When a person is *angry or frustrated*, he *slaps the back of the neck first*, and then *begins to rub it*. Those who *rub the backs of their necks* habitually, tend to be *critical* or *negative*.
- When a person has *forgotten to do a task assigned* to him, and when he is reminded of it, he invariably *slaps his forehead* or the *back of his head*, as if he were symbolically hitting himself. When he slaps his forehead, he blames himself for his forgetfulness.

Pain-in-the-neck gesture

Oh no!

When he slaps the back of his neck, he signals that you are a pain-in-the-neck for reminding him of his forgetfulness.
- Those who tend to *rub their foreheads* more often, are generally *easy-going people*.

Limb Barriers

Limbs act as barriers to protect a person from any hostile situation. It is natural for any human being to defend himself from averse circumstances by moving his limbs which becomes a way of expressing himself, complementing or supplementing his speech.

Folded Arms Gestures

As one grows older, one tends to cross one's arms more frequently. This forms a barrier, acting as a shield against an impending threat or a hostile situation, suggesting that he is *nervous, negative or defensive.*

- By folding his arms, a person pays less attention to what the speaker is saying.
- One may feel comfortable with one's arms crossed, simply because he has a defensive, negative or nervous attitude.

Standard Arm-Cross

In this gesture, both arms are folded together across the chest as a defence against an unfavourable situation.

The three common forms of the arm-cross gestures are: *the universal gesture, the reinforced arm-cross and the arm-gripping gesture.*

- The standard *universal arm-cross gesture* signifies the same defensive or negative attitude almost everywhere.

Standard arm-cross

Reinforced arm-cross

- When the arm-cross gesture is *reinforced* by clenched fists, it indicates a hostile and defensive attitude, ready for a physical assault.

Arms-grip

- In the case where the arm-cross gesture is complemented by the hands tightly *gripping the arms,* it shows a negative restrained attitude, commonly seen among patients sitting in the doctors' waiting room.

This universal gesture is commonly seen among strangers in public meetings, elevators, queues, cafeterias, etc, showing their uncertainty and insecurity.

Most people who *disagree* with what they are hearing, also take an *arms-folded position*. Status can also influence arm-folding gestures.

As long as the arms-folded gesture remains, the negative attitude will remain. An effective and simple way of breaking this gesture, is to hand a pen or a book to the person with crossed arms, so that it forces him to unfold his arms to reach forward for the object.

- In the *superior type of arm-crossing*, both thumbs point vertically upwards, signifying that the user is cool and self-confident, with the folded arms giving him a feeling of protection.

Superior attitude

Partial Arm-Cross Barrier

- A subtler form of arm-cross gesture is the partial one, in which *one arm swings across the body and holds or touches the other arm to form the barrier*, often seen at

meetings where the person may be a stranger to the group.
- Another partial form of arm-cross barrier *is holding one hand with the other,* commonly used by people who stand before a crowd, waiting to receive an award, or waiting to give a speech.

Partial arm-cross barrier

Holding hands

Disguised Arm-Cross Gestures

- These sophisticated gestures are used by people who are being continually exposed to others, eg, politicians, media persons, sales people, etc

Disguised nervousness

- Like the other arm-cross gestures, *one arm swings in the front of the body* but instead of grasping the other arm, *grasps some object* like a book, a handbag, a watch, a tie, a bracelet, etc

In this gesture, you will find the person adjusting his cuff-links or watch, or opening the handbag and checking its contents, etc, as *a cover for* his *nervousness*. It is also common to see people who are nervous, or unsure of themselves, holding their drinks with both hands.

This gesture can be observed in one who is trying to seek introduction to a pretty face, or one who is about to make his maiden speech in front of a large audience.

Cross-Legged Gestures

The cross-legged gesture also indicates a state of negative or defensive attitude. However, the crossed-arm gesture indicates a more defensive attitude than a cross-legged gesture.

The two basic cross-legged positions are the *standard leg-cross* and the *American position*.

- In the *standard leg-cross position*, one leg is crossed neatly over the other, and may be used to indicate a nervous, defensive or reserved attitude.

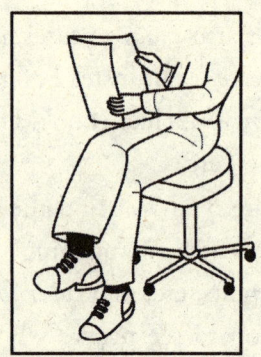

Standard leg-cross

But this gesture is usually a complementary gesture, and should not be interpreted in isolation. The situation must be taken into account, eg when people are sitting during lectures, or are seated too long on uncomfortable chairs and during cold weather.

- When this gesture is *accompanied by crossed arms*, it indicates that the person has withdrawn from the conversation. Women show their displeasure towards a husband or boyfriend by adopting this gesture.

Woman showing displeasure

- The *American position* is a leg-lock gesture that resembles the number four (4). This gesture indicates an argumentative or competitive attitude.

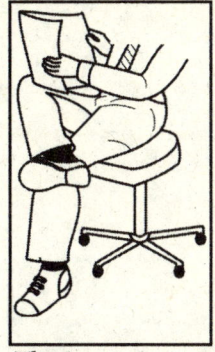
The American position

 When a person has an uncompromising attitude in a debate or argument, he assumes the American position and holds the crossed leg with both hands like a clamp, portraying himself to be a tough-minded and a stubborn person.

Leg-hands clamp

- Usually, when a person feels extremely *cold*, he will *fold his arms in a body hug*, and *cross his legs* which are generally straight, stiff and pressed hard against each other, unlike the relaxed leg posture of the defensive position.

Defensive standing position

- In a group, where each is a stranger to the other, you will usually find all the individuals standing with their *arms and legs crossed*, their *coats or jackets usually buttoned*, and bodies slightly stiff.

  In a group where everyone knows the other, you will generally see the

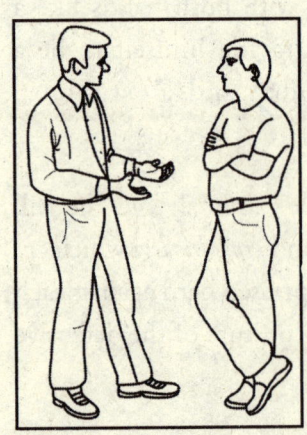

Open and closed body attitude

people with their *arms uncrossed, palms exposed, coats unbuttoned and leaning on one foot.*

Ankle-Lock

The ankle-lock also suggests a *negative or defensive attitude.*

Males generally *clench their fists on their knees or grip the arms of the chair while their ankles are locked,* suggesting a defensive or a negative attitude, or holding back an emotion.

Ankle lock – male version

Ankle lock – female version

Females may *hold their knees together, feet to one side, hands resting side by side, or one on top of the other on the lap.*

Foot-Lock

- This gesture is almost exclusively prominent in women who are shy or timid. When she *locks one foot around the other leg in a defensive attitude,* it indicates that she likes to be in her own shell.

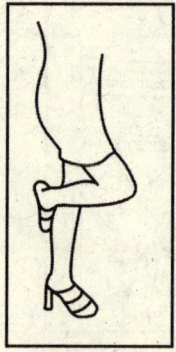

Standing foot-lock

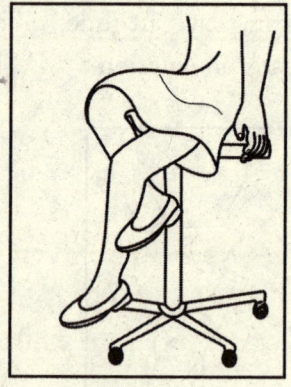

Sitting foot-lock

Eye Signals

Eyes are usually said to be the windows to one's soul. They may reveal the most accurate of all human communication signals as the pupils work independently, being a focal point of the body.

When one is excited, one's eyes dilate four times, whereas, they contract into beady eyes when one is angry or suspicious.

A person needing constant attention has dilated eyes, as they attempt to look appealing.

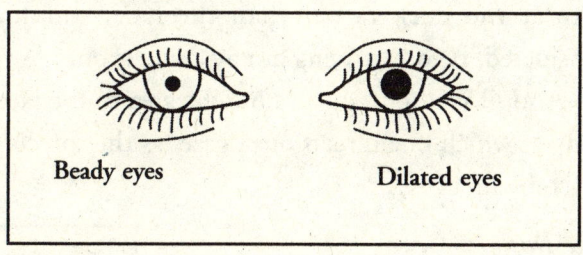

Eye signals

Gaze Behaviour

A dishonest person generally cannot meet another's eyes for long, probably holding the gaze less than one-third of the normal time.

A person who finds you appealing, interesting, or attractive, can hold your gaze for more than two-thirds of the time, and his eyes are dilated.

A person who wishes to issue a non-verbal challenge due to his hostility towards you, will have his eyes contracted and can also hold your gaze for a long time.

During negotiations, it is wiser to avoid having dealings with persons donning dark glasses, as you cannot read their reactions, nor should you wear one, for the other person feels you are staring at him unnecessarily.

Cultural customs, like the habit of the Japanese to gaze at the neck rather than the face, should be considered, before arriving at any conclusion.

Also, it is important to note the area of the face or body at which one directs one's gaze, as this affects the outcome of a deal.

The Business Gaze

While discussing business, imagine *a triangle on the other person's forehead*, and keep your gaze directed to this area to create a serious atmosphere that

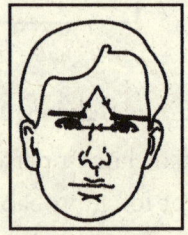

The business gaze

means business. As long as your gaze does not drop below the level of the others' eyes, you will be able to maintain control of the interaction.

The Social Gaze

To develop a social atmosphere, one needs to drop one's gaze below the other person's eye level. During such social encounters also, the gazer's eyes are *focused on a triangular area, which in this case, lies between the eyes and the mouth*.

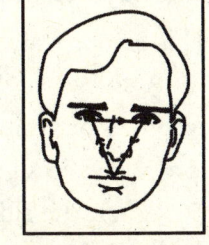
The social gaze

The Intimate Gaze

The intimate gaze *focuses across the eyes and below the chin* to other parts of the body. When you are close, the gaze is on the *triangular area between the eyes and the chest or breast*. When the encounter is distant, the gaze is between the eyes and the crotch.

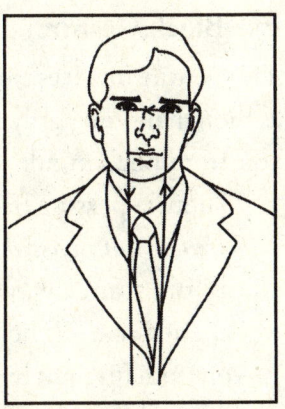
The intimate gaze

A person who wants to play hard, uses the social gaze rather than the intimate gaze.

Sideways Glance

This glance usually indicates either *interest or hostility.*

A sideways glance accompanied by slightly raised eyebrows or a smile, shows interest. It is especially used as a courtship signal.

When the sideways glance combines with a frown or the corners of the mouth turned down, it denotes hostility or suspicion or a critical attitude.

Eye Block Gesture

This gesture involves closing one's eyes for a few seconds, as though momentarily erasing you from one's mind.

- When a person becomes *bored or uninterested* in you or in some way feels superior to you, he blocks you from his sight by *closing his eyelids* and letting it remain so, for a few seconds.

Shutting out all

- When a person feels *superior* to you, the *head is tilted backwards accompanied by the eye block gesture* which gives you the impression that he is 'looking down his nose' with his long look.

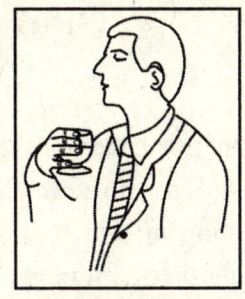

Eye block gesture

- For effective communication to take place, one needs to adopt a new approach instead of the eye block gesture that emits negative vibes.

Other Popular Gestures

In this chapter is discussed, a few common gestures which non-verbally communicate a lot of things, knowing which, a person will be able to comprehend another person, merely through his body-language.

Straddling a Chair

- When a person is *under physical or verbal attack,* he normally straddles a chair, for the back of the chair acts as a shield to his body.
- Most chair-straddlers are *aggressive and dominant,* trying to take control of people in a group who are bored, and the back of the chair acts as a barrier guarding against any attack from the group.

Straddling a chair

- To disarm such a person, it would be prudent to stand behind him, forcing him to change his position, and thus making him vulnerable.

    If the person is sitting on a swivel chair, then stand above and look down upon him, thus disconcerting him.

Picking Imaginary Lint

When *a person does not agree with the opinions of others,* but feels compelled to give his opinion, he will be seen picking imaginary pieces of lint from his clothing.

Lint-picking

This gesture is complemented by the person usually looking away from the others towards the floor.

Head Gestures

- The head *nod* is a popular gesture universally, signifying 'yes'. The head sideways *shake*, is also a popular universal gesture, meaning 'no'.

Neutral head position

- When a person has a *neutral* attitude about what he is hearing, he keeps his *head held up;* and nods occasionally.
- When he *tilts* his head to one side, he is showing *interest* in what he hears. Women often use this position of interest when they are interested in an attractive male.
- A *negative and judgmental* attitude is indicated when the head is kept *down*.

Interested position

Disapproval position

Hands Behind the Head

People such as lawyers, managers, other professionals generally use this gesture of keeping *both hands behind the head,* showing their *confidence, superiority or dominance.*

This is also common with those who have the know-it-all attitude which can be quite irritating to many people.

Lawyers generally use this gesture with their peers to prove their knowledgeability.

Also, a person who stakes a claim to a particular area, is seen using such a gesture.

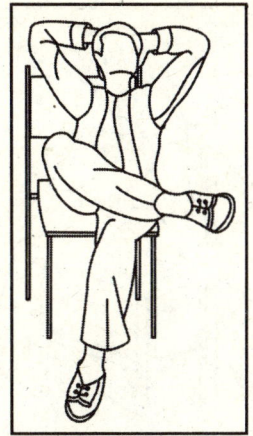

Hands behind head

A good method of handling this gesture is to force the person to change his position, by placing something in front of him, but just beyond his reach, and asking, "Have you seen this?" This will force him to unclasp his hands from behind his head and lean forward to pick up the object.

Another way is to copy his gesture, showing that you are as smart as he is, like most lawyers do.

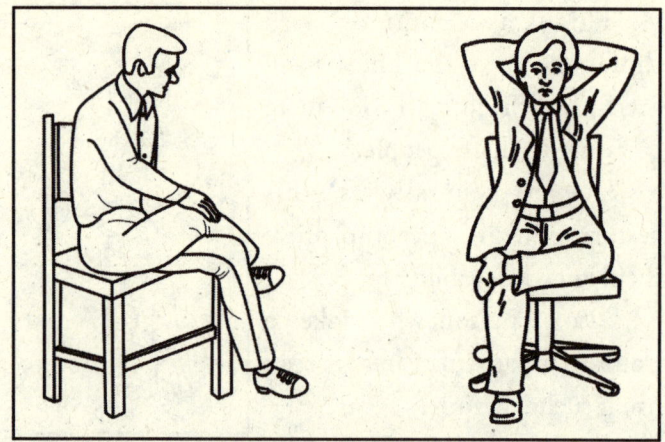

Copying the gesture

Aggressive and Readiness Gestures

The most common aggressive gesture is *putting one's hands on one's hips,* showing *a readiness for the act.* A person who uses this gesture is ready to tackle his objectives and goals, and so this gesture is also termed as the achiever stance.

Ready for action

- Men often use this stance in the presence of the fairer sex to show their dominant and aggressive attitude.

- Men also use this gesture as a non-verbal challenge to other men.
- When a person wears a closed coat and assumes this posture, he shows an aggressive frustration, while when a man wears an open coat which is pushed back, he shows a non-verbal display of fearlessness.
- Professional models use this aggressive readiness gesture to make the clothing he or she is displaying, appear more appealing.

Professional model's stance

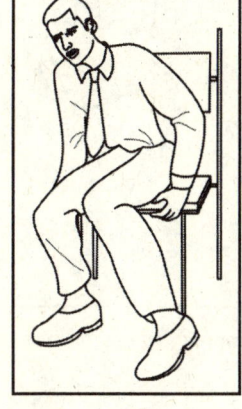

Ready to proceed

Seated Readiness

In the seated readiness gesture, a *negotiator* can assess a potential buyer's interest in the product. When a person, after stroking his chin while making a discussion, chooses to adopt the seated-readiness gesture, then one can be sure of a positive answer from him, whereas if he crosses his arms after making his decision, the response from him would be negative.

An *angry person* who wishes to throw someone out, also uses this gesture.

A person wishing to *end a conversation or an encounter*, sits with his hands on his knees, or on the edge of his chair with his body bent forward.

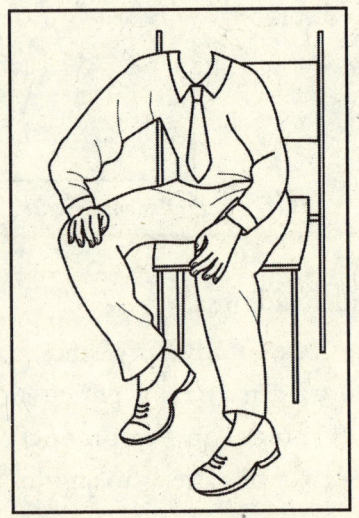

Ready to end conversation

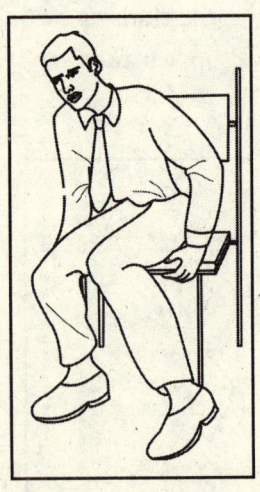

Ready to end encounter

Sexual Aggressiveness

A sexually aggressive attitude is displayed by *thumbs tucked into the belt or the pant pockets*, like cowboys do. In this gesture, the arms are in the readiness position, with the hands serving as the focal pointers. Men use this gesture with other men to show their fearlessness. In the presence of women, this gesture denotes dominance. When a woman wears a dress, she usually tucks a thumb into a belt or a pocket.

The cowboy stance

The sexually aggressive female

Aggression Between Men

When two men are unconsciously evaluating each other, they use the *hands-on-hips and thumbs-in-belt gestures,* both of them turned at an angle away from each other, with their lower halves of their bodies relaxed.

Evaluating each other

As long as their hands are on their hips, and open palm gestures are not used, a completely relaxed atmosphere will not be there, though their conversation may be casual or friendly.

Trouble brewing

A fight is likely to occur, if they are *directly facing each other,* with their feet firmly planted on the ground.

Gestures with Glasses

• The act of *putting objects,* like one arm of the spectacles or a pencil end *against the lips or in the mouth* is essentially a *reassurance or security gesture.*

- This also helps in stalling or *delaying a decision.*
- Removing and cleaning spectacles also serves as stalling methods.
- Looking over the top of the spectacles, rather than removing them, can be a costly mistake, because the person at the receiving end will inevitably react to this look with folded arms, crossed legs and a negative attitude.

Stalling for time

Looking over the glasses

Attitudes

Touch

A touch expresses one's attitude or frame of mind, and a desire to convey a message to another. When someone approaches you and touches you, it indicates that he wants you to stop and listen to him.

When a person grasps another's hand, the gesture is used to interrupt a conversation or to stress on some issue that arises in the conversation.

A touch is also used as a gesture for pacifying someone in distress.

Boredom

- A person may be looking into your eyes and you get the impression that he is listening to you, but his unblinking eyes denote that he is sleeping with his eyes open, that is, he has a blank gaze, denoting boredom.
- Biting nails, yawning, frequent glances at the wristwatch, showing signs of hunger or thirst, are symptoms indicative of boredom.

Smoking

- A smoker generally covers up his anxiety by smoking.
- Pipe smokers use cleaning, lighting, tapping, filling, packing gestures most frequently during sales interviews to relieve tension, or tense moments. They like to stall decision-making, and they do it in a most unobtrusive and socially acceptable manner.

Positive attitude

- A cigarette smoker generally makes quicker decisions than a pipe smoker.
- A person feeling positive, confident and self-assured, generally blows the smoke in an upward direction most of the time, while one with a negative attitude, blows the smoke downwards most of the time.

Negative attitude

- A secretive attitude is indicated when a person blows out smoke from the corner of his mouth.
- The faster the person blows smoke upwards or downwards, the more positive or negative a person's attitude is.

- Blowing out smoke through the nostrils is a sign of a superior, confident individual.
- The continuous tapping of a cigar or cigarette end on the ashtray is indicative of an inner conflict.
- When a person wishes to terminate a conversation, he will light a cigarette and suddenly extinguish it.

Courtship Gestures

People who are successful in sexual encounters with members of the opposite sex, have the ability to send courtship signals and to be aware of those being reciprocated. Men are far less perceptive than women, regarding courtship and other body gestures. Some courtship gestures are studied and deliberate, while others are given unconsciously.

- Certain changes are observed when a man and a woman approach each other from a distance, eg body sagging disappears, chest protrudes, stomach is pulled in, potbellied slumping disappears, the body becomes erect, the person appears to become more youthful.

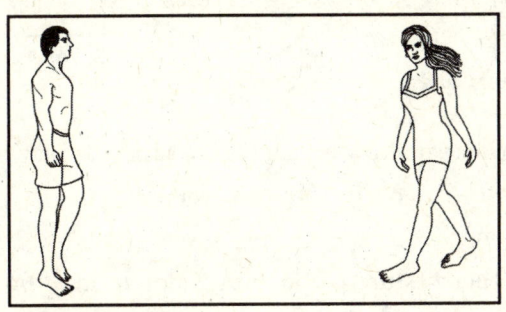

Approaching each other

- The best place to study these changes is the beach. Most often, a person returns to his original posture after he has passed the person who attracted his attention.

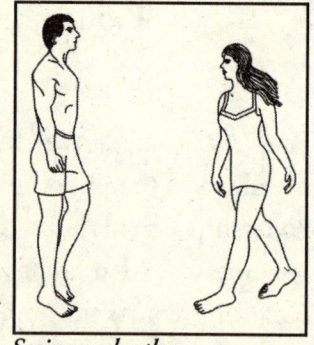
Seeing each other

Male Courtship Gestures

- Men like to preen when they see a female approaching them, and you will find them *straightening their tie* or *their collar,* or *brushing away imaginary dust from their shoulder,* or *rearranging their coat or shirt or even their hair.*

Male preening gesture

- A male may show his aggressive sexual display by the *thumbs-in-belt gesture* that focuses on his genital region.
- Another gesture could be that of *turning his body towards the female, and pointing his foot at her.*

- He will *hold her gaze intimately* for a split second longer than necessary or usual, with his pupils dilated.
- Often, you see a man with his *hands on his hips*, a gesture to show off his physique and his willingness to get involved with the female in front.
- While leaning against a wall, or while seated, he may *spread out his legs* to attract attention.
- Men are guileless and less subtle than women, when it comes to displaying their courtship gestures.

Female courtship gestures

Like men, women too like to preen, touching their hair, smoothening their clothing, placing one or both hands on their hips, pointing out a foot towards the male, gazing intimately and increasing the gaze hold.

Female preening gesture

- A women's *one thumb-in-belt gesture* is more subtle and feminine. She might also tuck in one thumb into her pocket, and allow it to protrude from her handbag.

- She too *has pupil dilation* when excited, compounded with *flushed cheeks*.
- Women like to *toss their hair back over the shoulder or away from their face,* including those women who sport short hair.
- An interested female will *expose the soft, smooth skin of her wrists*, considered to be one of the highly erotic areas of the body, to the potential male partner. She may also expose her palm while speaking.
- While sitting or standing, a female may tend to *keep her leg open wider* than normally done, when a male arrives on the scene.

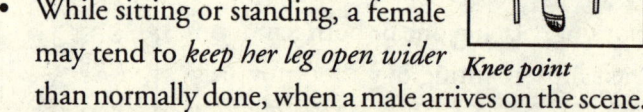
Knee point

- She has an *accentuated roll of the pelvic region while walking*.
- She *holds the man's gaze, with her eyelids partially drooping*, long enough for him to notice, before she looks away.
- She *wets her lips*, thereby denoting sexual invitation.
- The colour of the *lipstick* is used to indicate a sexually aroused woman.

- *Fondling objects* like the stem of a glass, a cigarette, the strap of a handbag, etc, may indicate the thoughts running through her mind.
- A woman may display her courtship gesture by *tucking one leg under the other, and pointing the knee to the person she is interested in.*
- The *shoe fondle* by thrusting the foot in and out of the shoe can arouse some men sexually.

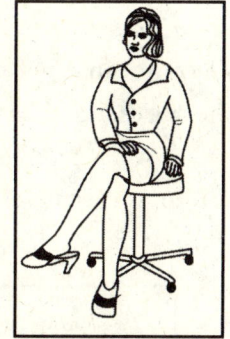

Shoe fondle

- The *leg twine* or *the crossing of one leg over the other*, is the most enticing sitting position that a woman can take to attract attention.

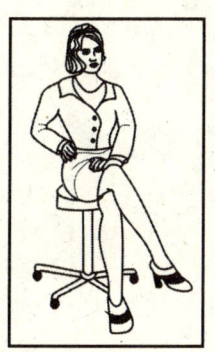

Leg twine

- Some women indulge in crossing and uncrossing the legs slowly before a man, while gently stroking the thighs with her hand, indicating a fond wish to be touched.

Territorial and Ownership Gestures

Territorial Gestures

People *leaning against objects* or other people, claim territorial rights on them, showing thereby their *dominance*. When a person touches a property, it becomes an extension of his body, thereby showing that he stakes a claim to it.

Lovers may have their *arms around their beloved*, business executives may place their *feet on their desk*, or *lean against their office doorway*.

Showing pride of ownership

A person can intimidate another by abusing his territory, eg, borrowing his car, or sitting at his desk without permission.

Ownership Gestures

People in high positions use the ownership gesture more frequently.

The *leg-over-chair gesture* signifies the man's ownership of that particular chair, though by doing this, he may also reflect an easy-going, relaxed and carefree attitude. This attitude may

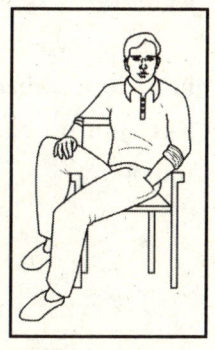

Lack of concern

Claiming ownership of desk

show his lack of concern when he adopts this posture in front of his employee who is seated before him with a problem.

If the chair has no arms, it is quite likely that the person may plant both his *feet on the desk,* thus claiming ownership.

When his boss enters, the seated man may use subtler means of claiming possession, by discreetly placing one foot on the bottom drawer of the desk, or against the leg of the desk.

The way to disturb such a stance of the person is to hand him something that he cannot reach, which will force him to plant his feet on the ground to reach for the object.

Mirror Images

When a person uses gestures and postures identical to the person to whom he is talking, it indicates mutual liking and agreement in matters of common interest. This copying is common among friends, those from the same status and married couples. Sometimes, identical gestures reflect a non-verbal challenge.

In agreement

Non-verbal challenge

An employee may copy his boss's gestures to influence a face-to-face encounter, as this puts the boss in a receptive and relaxed frame of mind. But, this copying of gestures may not always work for the employee, especially, when his superior adopts a dominant and competitive attitude, by adopting a T-cross gesture and a 4-leg-lock figure.

Copying for gaining acceptance

One generally sees lawyers, accountants, leaders and management personnel assuming these postures in front of people they consider 'inferior'.

Leaders tend to be the first of a group to walk through a doorway, and they normally sit at the end of a sofa or couch, rather than in the centre.

Pointers

There are times when a person to whom you are talking, shows subtly that he would rather be elsewhere than with you, even though he looks like enjoying your company. Though the person's head is turned towards you, and he is smiling and nodding, yet his body and feet are pointing away from you, either towards another person, or towards an exit, showing what his desire is.

Body showing mind's desire

When you see a person turning his body away from you, you must realise that he is losing interest in you.

Open Formation

Many people position their bodies at an angle to give non-verbal clues to others.

Two people angle their bodies in such a way as if an imaginary third person is also with them. This formation, serves as a non-verbal invitation for a third person to join in the conversation at the third point.

When a fourth person joins in, a square is formed. When there are more than four persons, then a circle is formed.

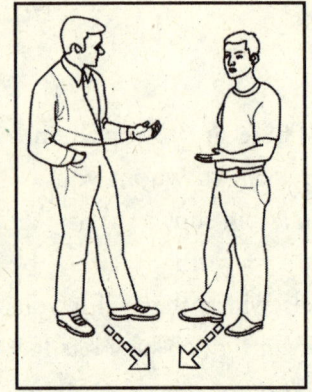
Open triangular formation

Closed Formation

When two people are involved in an intimate or private conversation, then they face each other directly.

- A suitor will *point his body towards the woman, facing her directly,* gradually closing the distance between them as he moves into her intimate zone.

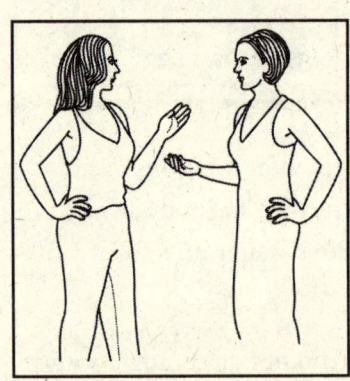
Closed formation

- In a closed formation, the distance between two people is usually less than that of the open formation. The closed formation

can also be used as a non-verbal challenge between people who are hostile to each other.
- If two people are interested in each other, they may *mirror each other's gestures.*

Inclusion-Exclusion Techniques

Both the open triangular and the closed formation stops another person from joining the group or their conversation.

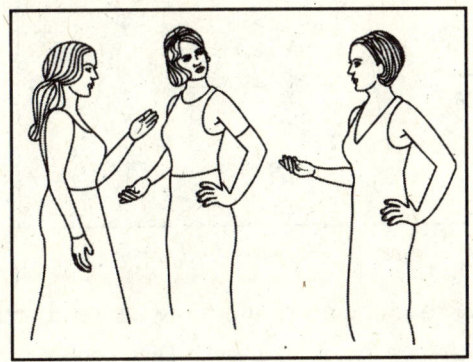

Third person unwanted

When *two people are in a closed formation, and a third wishes to join* in, the other two have to orient their bodies so as *to form a triangle.*

When a *third person is unwanted,* the two in the closed formation will merely *turn their heads, and not their bodies.*

Seated Body Pointing

When a person is interested in another person, or accepts another, he *crosses his knees towards him/her*. If the other reciprocates the interest or acceptance, he too will cross his knees towards the first person.

Body pointing to exclude the third person

As they become more and more involved with each other, their gestures and movements become similar, and a closed formation results.

If *another person* wants to join this formation, he has to position himself in such a manner that a *triangle is formed*.

Interviewing Two People

During an interview involving the interviewer and two people to be interviewed, when one person is very talkative and the other reserved, you can involve both of them by turning your attention continually from one person to the other.

Foot Pointing

The feet serve as *pointers to the direction in which a person would like to go.*

In a group, where three men and a very attractive woman are conversing, with the men dominating the conversation, you will

Foot pointers denoting

notice that all men have one foot pointing towards the woman, showing their interest in her.

The woman, in turn, may point one foot towards the one she is interested in.

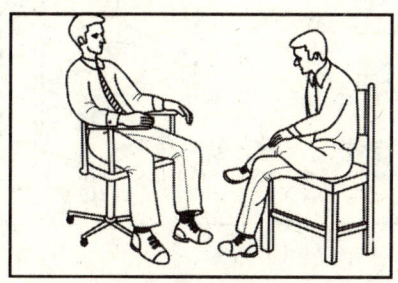

Open triangular formation

Seated Body Formations

The *open triangular formation,* like the standing position, gives an *informal,* relaxed attitude to a meeting, in which the boss can open a counselling session with his employee, whose performance has been unsatisfactory.

The boss can show non-verbal agreement with his employee from this position by copying his movements and gestures.

When there is mutual agreement, both their bodies will point to form a triangular movement.

- When a person wants direct answers to his questions, he points his *body directly* at his subordinate by turning his chair likewise, indicating non-verbally, his intentions.

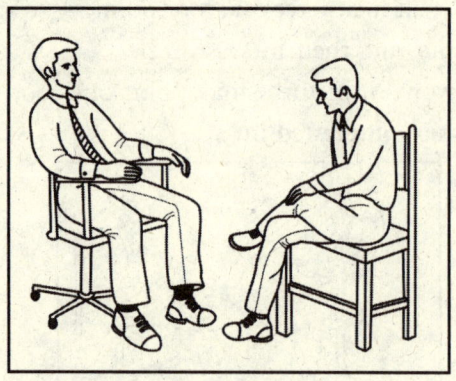

Right angle formation

- By positioning his *body at a right angle* away from his employee, the boss takes the pressure off the interview.

    The right angle formation encourages more open answers to one's questions, even if they are delicate or embarrassing questions.

    The right angle position allows the other person to think and act independently, as the pressure eases.

Influence of Spatial Zones and Culture on Body Language

Like many animals, humans have created their own spatial zones to mark and identify specific areas while interacting with or defending themselves against other individuals. The five spatial zones are:
- Close intimate zone – 0-6 in (See 1)
- Intimate zone – 6 in 1= ft. 6 in (See 2)
- Personal zone – 1 ft. 6 in - 4 ft (See 3)
- Social zone – 4 - 12 ft. (See 4)
- Public zone – 12 ft. + (See 5)

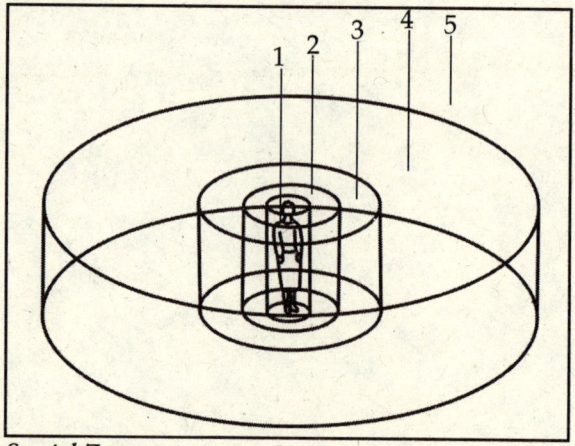

Spatial Zones

These zonal demarcations tend to vary when people from different cultures meet, as their spatial needs and assumptions differ.

- A North American or a West European who greets with an outstretched handshake, gets confused when greeted with a hug from a Latin American business colleague.

Outstretched handshake

A hug

- A Korean business person, schooled to maintain space, feels comfortable if his Western counterpart shakes his hand firmly from a distance, looking straight into his eyes.
- *Salaam* is the traditional greeting used in Arabic-speaking and Islamic countries.
- *Namaste* is the recognised gesture of greeting in India,

when both hands are held up in front of the chest with palms together and a slight bow.
- Bowing is the traditional form of greeting in Japan. A formal bow is when the body bends forward by about 30 degrees and the palms of the hands are placed on the knees, while in an informal one the body inclines at about 15 degrees and the hands are kept at the sides.

Despite cultural variations, when we meet or leave someone, we reveal through certain gestures that our intentions towards the other person are amicable. *A broad smile, flashing of the eyes* and *shooting up of the eyebrows*, with a *wrinkling of the forehead*, clubbed with *hailing, waving* and *handshaking* are recognition signals, which form an integral part of universally accepted greetings.

Conclusion

The complex human body language is a result of the gradual changes that have emerged out of an evolutionary process beginning from fish, to amphibians and reptiles, to mammals. It is largely from the prehistoric apes, the close kin to the living chimpanzee, that we humans derive our tendency to express through gestures. Hence, like humans, apes and monkeys snarl with rage showing their front teeth, raise their eyebrows when frightened, use the thumbs and fingers to grasp and seize food when hungry.

In human beings, non-vocal communication has been replaced by speech through evolution, and body language remains to reinforce and complement spoken statements, to replace spoken statements (if, for example, secrecy is needed), to express one's feelings and opinions and as a means of greeting. So, when you are asked how people communicate with one another, do not just say, with words, but also mention the unspoken language of the body and the face.

Having dealt with the body and facial gestures, I would like to conclude with a concise table showing gestures corresponding to particular emotions, which will help the readers to interpret and comprehend body language at a quick glance.

Body Language, as you must be aware of by now, is a complex interaction of hand, leg and body gestures, along with facial expressions. Careful and systematic study of each of these will enable you to understand what a person expresses non-verbally, and therefore help you act accordingly.